W9-AVS-740

Franklin and the Duckling

From an episode of the animated TV series *Franklin,*
produced by Nelvana Limited, Neurones France s.a.r.l. and
Neurones Luxembourg S.A, based on the Franklin books
by Paulette Bourgeois and Brenda Clark.

Story written by Sharon Jennings
Illustrated by Sean Jeffrey, Sasha McIntyre and Jelena Sisic.
Based on the TV episode *Franklin and the Duckling,* written by Nicola Barton.

Kids Can Read is a registered trademark of Kids Can Press Ltd.

Franklin

Franklin is a trademark of Kids Can Press Ltd.
The character of Franklin was created by Paulette Bourgeois and Brenda Clark.
Text © 2007 Contextx Inc.
Illustrations © 2007 Brenda Clark Illustrator Inc.

Kids Can Press acknowledges the financial support of the Government of Ontario,
through the Ontario Media Development Corporation's Ontario Book Initiative; the
Ontario Arts Council; the Canada Council for the Arts; and the Government of
Canada, through the BPIDP, for our publishing activity.

Published in Canada by
Kids Can Press Ltd.
29 Birch Avenue
Toronto, ON M4V 1E2

Published in the U.S. by
Kids Can Press Ltd.
2250 Military Road
Tonawanda, NY 14150

www.kidscanpress.com

Series editor: Tara Walker
Edited by Jennifer Stokes
Designed by Céleste Gagnon

Printed and bound in China

The hardcover edition of this book is smyth sewn casebound.
The paperback edition of this book is limp sewn with a drawn-on cover.

CM 07 0 9 8 7 6 5 4 3 2 1
CM PA 07 0 9 8 7 6 5 4 3 2 1

Library and Archives Canada Cataloguing in Publication

Jennings, Sharon
    Franklin and the duckling / written by Sharon Jennings ;
illustrated by Sean Jeffrey, Sasha McIntyre, Jelena Sisic.

(Kids Can read)
The character Franklin was created by Paulette Bourgeois and Brenda Clark.

ISBN-13: 978-1-55337-888-4 (bound) ISBN-10: 1-55337-888-1 (bound)
ISBN-13: 978-1-55337-889-1 (pbk.) ISBN-10: 1-55337-889-X (pbk.)

1. Ducklings–Juvenile fiction. I. Jeffrey, Sean II. McIntyre, Sasha
III. Sisic, Jelena IV. Bourgeois, Paulette V. Clark, Brenda VI. Title.
VII. Series: Kids Can read (Toronto, Ont.)

PS8569.E563F7157 2007   jC813'.54   C2005-902222-1

Kids Can Press is a l'oгus™ Entertainment company

Franklin and the Duckling

Kids Can Press

Franklin can tie his shoes.

Franklin can count by twos.

And Franklin can take good care

of his pet goldfish, Goldie.

Now, Franklin wants another pet.

This is a problem.

His mother says, "No more pets!"

One day, Franklin and Bear

went to the pond.

They swam back and forth.

They did swan dives

and cannonballs.

Then they heard a sound.

QUACK!

Franklin looked around.

QUACK! QUACK!

"It's a baby duck!" said Franklin.

QUACK!

The duckling swam right to Franklin.

All afternoon, the duckling

stayed with Franklin.

He swam when

Franklin swam.

He dived when

Franklin dived.

He splashed when Franklin splashed.

"Maybe he thinks you're his mother,"

said Bear.

"Hmmm," said Franklin.

"Where *is* his mother?"

Franklin and Bear looked all around.

They did not see any other ducks.

"I know!" said Franklin.

"I will take him

home with me.

I really want another pet."

Bear shook his head.

"Your mom said no more pets,

remember?"

Franklin sighed.

"I remember," he said.

Soon, it was time for supper.

Bear hurried home.

Franklin turned to the duckling.

"I can't have another pet," he said.

"But I'll be back tomorrow."

Franklin walked

up the hill.

Franklin crossed

the meadow.

Franklin turned

in at the gate.

Franklin opened

his front door.

QUACK!

He looked

behind him.

Franklin picked up the duckling.

QUACK!

QUACK!

"Shhhh!"

said Franklin.

He put the duckling in his cap.

He ran to his bedroom.

"Do you want

to be my pet?"

asked Franklin.

QUACK!

"Shhhh!" said Franklin again.

"You have to be my *secret* pet."

Franklin got to work.

He got his wading pool and filled

it with water.

He made a nest

with mud and leaves.

He found lots

of bugs and flies.

"There," said Franklin. "Just like home."

QUACK!

Franklin's mother knocked on his door.

"Suppertime!" she called.

QUACK!

Franklin opened his door.

He closed it behind him.

"Did I hear a duck?" asked his mother.

"No," fibbed Franklin.

"I coughed."

QUACK! QUACK!

"See?" said Franklin.

"COUGH! COUGH!"

"Hmmm," said
Franklin's mother.

Franklin ate his supper super fast.

He hurried back to his room.

"Oh, no!" cried Franklin.

Everything was wet.

Everything was muddy.

And the duckling was chewing

Franklin's homework!

Franklin tried to tidy up.

Then he yawned and went to bed.

QUACK!

QUACK!

"Shhhh!"

said Franklin.

He read the

duckling a story.

He sang the

duckling a song.

"Now go to sleep," he said.

But the duckling didn't want to go to sleep.

QUACK!

QUACK!

QUACK!

Franklin put on his earmuffs.

In the morning, Franklin's mother

knocked on his door.

"Breakfast!" she called.

QUACK!

Franklin opened his door.

He closed it behind him.

"Did I hear a duck?" asked his mother.

"No," fibbed Franklin.

"I sneezed."

QUACK!

QUACK!

"See?" said Franklin.

"ACHOO! ACHOO!"

"Hmmm," said

Franklin's mother.

Franklin sat down to eat.

Just then, Harriet came into the room.

She was holding
the duckling.
"Duck," she said.
"Duck go
quack quack."

Everyone looked at Franklin.

"I can explain," said Franklin.

Franklin explained.

Everyone followed Franklin

to his bedroom.

It was a bigger mess than before.

"A duckling isn't a pet,"

said Franklin's mother.

"A duckling is wild."

"I know that now," sighed Franklin.

Franklin picked up the duckling.

"Come on," he said.

"I'm taking you back to the pond."

But just then …

QUACK! QUACK! QUACK!

QUACK! QUACK! QUACK!

Franklin looked out the window.

Six ducks were on the lawn.

"Wow!" said Franklin.

"Your family has come to find you!"

The duckling looked
at Franklin.
QUACK! QUACK!
"Good-bye to you, too,"
said Franklin.

The duckling waddled
off to join his parents.

"You took good care of your duckling,"
said Franklin's mother.
"Maybe you are ready
for another pet."
And Franklin said …

"No! No more pets!"